Written by
Rachel Hurt

Edited by
Ryan Durney, Debra Hurt
& Bradley Wilson

Illustration, layout & design by
Ryan Durney

Guardians of the Forest © 2022 Rachel Hurt

2nd Edition   ISBN: 978-0-578-39648-4

To my family
For always supporting &
loving me. Thank you for
helping me every step of the way!

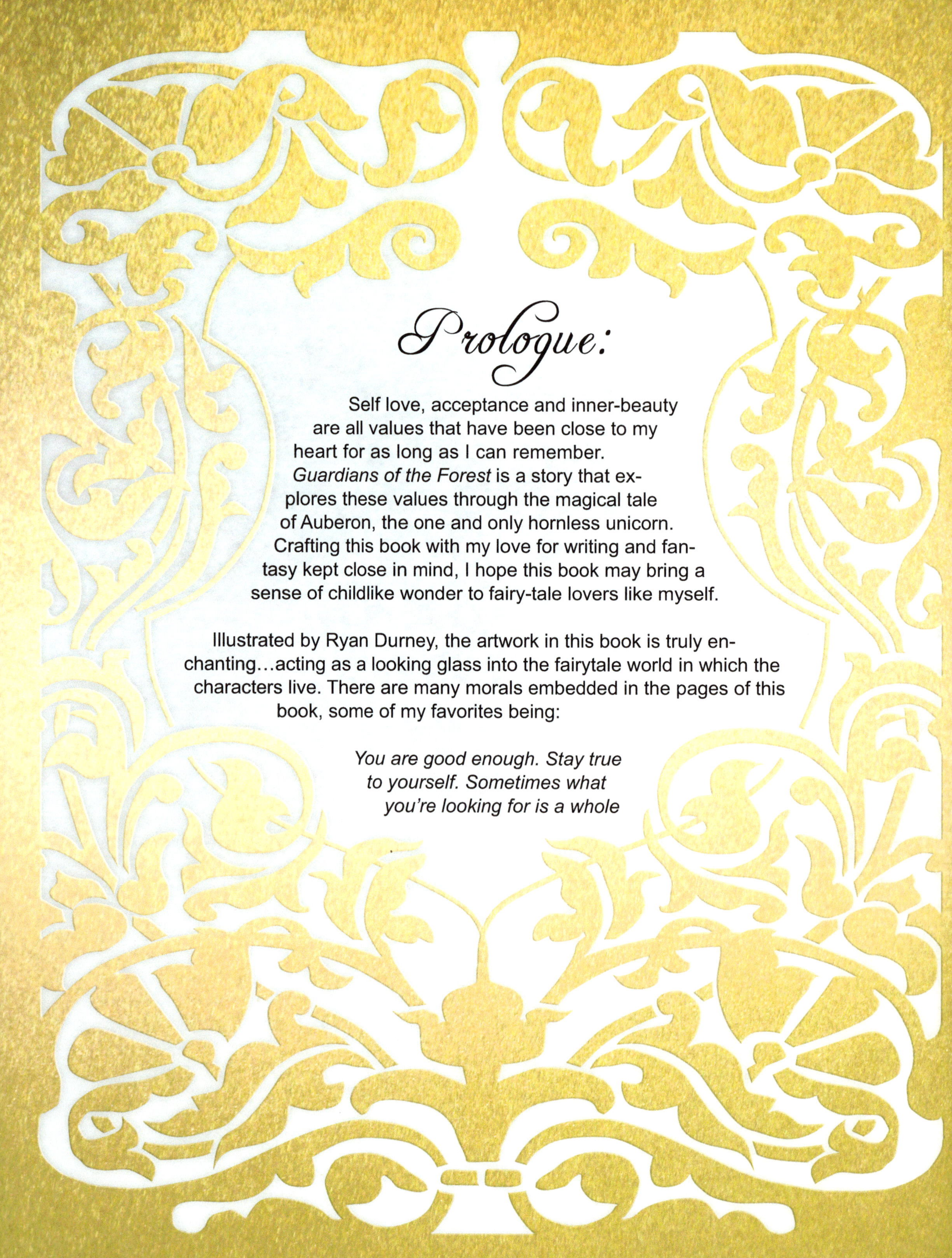

Prologue:

Self love, acceptance and inner-beauty
are all values that have been close to my
heart for as long as I can remember.
Guardians of the Forest is a story that ex-
plores these values through the magical tale
of Auberon, the one and only hornless unicorn.
Crafting this book with my love for writing and fantasy kept close in mind, I hope this book may bring a
sense of childlike wonder to fairy-tale lovers like myself.

Illustrated by Ryan Durney, the artwork in this book is truly en-
chanting…acting as a looking glass into the fairytale world in which the
characters live. There are many morals embedded in the pages of this
book, some of my favorites being:

*You are good enough. Stay true
to yourself. Sometimes what
you're looking for is a whole*

lot closer than you think. Self-acceptance and self-love are some of the most important values. Release your inner beauty.

Originally sold and printed for a limited edition series, I successfully reached my goal of selling 1,000 signed and numbered copies. 100% of the proceeds from these copies were donated to the Andy Roddick Foundation, which was a sum of $16,174. Now, after much time, effort, and preparation, I am excited to announce the launch of my 2nd Edition copy and its publication to be sold on many platforms in the near future! The beautiful story of *Guardians of the Forest* rings true to my heart, and I truly hope you cherish it as much as I do.

With love, Rachel

Guardians of the Forest

By Rachel Hurt

Illustration by Ryan Durney

Unicorn

grove

Once upon a time...

there was a forest, but not just any ordinary forest. This forest was full of grand, old trees, with chocolate-brown bark and shimmering cinnamon branches. Their rustling fingers reached into the sky.

Many creatures lived in their forest, but the unicorns were the most magnificent of them all. And favored by a grove of the oldest oak trees, who were known as the Guardians of the Forest. These trees had special ways of communicating, so they saw and heard every little thing that happened under their crowns. They never tired of watching the marvelous and graceful unicorns at play. The clip-clopping sound of unicorn hooves made their leaves flutter happily in the soft breeze.

However, there was one unicorn in particular that caught the Oldest Oak Tree's eyes, as he was different from the rest. Throughout the lands, Auberon was known as the only horn-less unicorn.

Because he had no horn, other forest animals liked to pick on him. Auberon was fed up with all of the animals chit-chattering behind his back about how different he was. So one day he decided to do something about it. Auberon traveled to a grove of trees rumored to possess unusual magic. As he arrived, an old and wrinkly face appeared on the grandest oak in the grove. Suddenly, the Oak's bark face stretched its jaw, cracking it in different directions until it could speak in a way that a unicorn could understand. It had been a long time since the Oldest Oak had revealed its face.

Auberon stomped impatiently. "It's about time I got my horn!" he thought. This could be his only chance at being normal.

"I have heard that you can do magical things. So, I've come for you to give me a horn," Auberon said, matter-of-factly.

The tree raised his eyebrows, and his whole face
made noises, as he was thinking.

"Let me see… uhhhhhh… no," the tree said firmly.

"No? Well, why not?" Auberon asked. "Out of unicorns big and small, who live near and far, I'm the only one who doesn't have a horn. Don't you think that's just a little bit unfair? I mean, after all, I am a unicorn, and what's a unicorn without a horn?"

"Mmmmm," the tree sighed. "So you must have a horn to be yourself?"

"Well...yes, I'm a unicorn. I need a horn. Each and every day I get picked on and teased because I don't have a horn. Having a horn would be my happily ever after. I'm just really hoping that you might give me one?" he said, wishing that the tree would understand.

"Auberon, listen closely… I would like to give you a horn, but that doesn't mean I'm going to. If I granted all the wishes in the forest, then the squirrels would have pouches and the rabbits would fly! If you really want a horn, then you must figure out how to get it on your own."

Auberon sighed. "I just don't understand. What do I have to do to get my horn?"

"That part is up to you to decide. But, remember, when an opportunity arises don't be afraid to go after it. And a simple piece of advice, if someone wants to make friends, don't turn them away because you are afraid that they will make fun of you. There are many creatures in these woods that would want to be your friend. All you have to do is give them a chance."

"Well, I doubt it…" Auberon mumbled. "But anyway, thanks for the help. I guess I'll see you around."

"Farewell, Auberon."

In the blink of an eye, before Auberon could say another word, he watched the Oldest Oak's face sink back into the tree bark. When Auberon turned around to leave, the faintest shadow of a smile rippled across the bark. This was going to be a great journey for Auberon, thought the tree.

Auberon went back to his grove, disheartened.

A tall and muscular unicorn, named Gideon, would often stand
with his shimmering gold horn over Auberon, acting superior.

"Look everybody," he would say. "It's the hornless unicorn!"

Then he would continue to prance around Auberon in a circle, snickering.

"He's probably going to stay hornless for the rest of his pathetic life, too."

The other unicorns and forest animals also mocked Auberon, sending unfriendly looks in his direction. He lowered his head, ashamed in the presence of the majestic unicorns around him. Gideon laughed sarcastically, and galloped off with the rest of the unicorns following him. The other forest creatures around Auberon laughed too, and soon all of them

left. All of the birds flew out of their nests, and all of the rabbits hopped away.

A little bluebird saw what had happened, and that Auberon was very sad. But nevertheless, he seemed friendly
enough, so she decided to go talk to him. She blew in the
wind, unaware that the trees were gently guiding her over
to Auberon. "Listen, I saw how those other unicorns were
mean to you, but I don't think being a hornless unicorn is a
bad thing," she said smiling at him warmly. He half-smiled,
then sighed. "A unicorn without a horn is just a horse," he
thought, glumly.

"I think you're perfect just the way you are. The other forest creatures just don't see it in you. That already makes you better than them. Unlike them, you can see what lies within, rather than what is found on the outside," she said, proud of her true words.

"Well, thanks, but there's not really much *we* can do about it. I'll never change. I mean, you're just a little bluebird, and me? I'm just a hornless unicorn. There's no possible chance of me ever fitting in." He stared at the ground with his head hung low.

"But you don't have to fit in," she said, flying closer to Auberon with a compassionate look in her eyes. "Anyways, fitting in is just another way of being the same as everyone else."

Auberon smiled, remembering what the tree had said. The little bluebird was only trying to help.

"Oh, I'm sorry," Auberon said, changing the subject. "I didn't introduce myself," he said. "I'm Auberon."

"Well, it's nice to meet you Auberon. I'm Willow," she said, with a little chirp.

"It's nice to meet you too, Willow," he said genuinely.
They then marched off together, down the mossy paths...

Throughout the next couple of days, Willow and Auberon enjoyed talking to each other. They had many conversations, and a beautiful friendship was being built. Willow was the first real friend Auberon had ever known. Finally he knew what friendship felt like, and he loved it!

One day Willow had a marvelous idea. She flew around him, sharing it.

"Maybe we should go to the Old Oak Trees. They have magical powers. Maybe *they* can give you a horn?"

"I have to admit it's a good idea, at least... it was. The only problem is I already tried that. They can be very stubborn, and don't grant wishes just like that," Auberon explained to her.

"Hmmmm... well, you know I've heard rumors of a witch's house hidden somewhere in this forest. Maybe we could travel there, and she could grant you a horn."

"Oh my gosh! Willow, that's a great idea," Auberon said excitedly.

Willow continued on with her plan. "We could ask any Old Oak Trees that we find for directions to get there. I'm sure they will tell us. Plus, there's one tree that is particularly good with directions. She's very tall compared to the rest, so she can see much farther than the others. Why don't we ask her?"

"Yes, that's brilliant! All this time of being teased and... Wow, you're a genius! I can't believe I didn't think of that before," Auberon said.

Once they reached the grove of trees, Willow led Auberon to the tree that she had spoken of.

"Why hello, Willow," the Lady Oak Tree said, with a friendly welcoming.

"Hello!" Willow said cheerfully.

"What a lovely surprise, and I see you've brought a friend."

"Yes, this is my friend Auberon," she said.

"Hi," Auberon said.

"Hello. Nice to meet you Auberon," the Lady Oak Tree said greeting him, though she already knew who he was.

"We've come to ask you for directions to the witch's house, in hopes that the witch will be able to give him his horn," Willow said.

She continued, "You see, my friend Auberon here, is actually not a horse at all. But in fact, he's a unicorn."

Auberon nodded along in agreement.

The Lady Oak Tree laughed quietly to herself, for she already knew this, then said, "You've brought your friend to the right place, Willow." Looking over her shoulder, all of her branches turned towards the direction of the witch's house. "Go this way," she said. "You'll know you're on the right path when you come across a meadow with a bridge in it."

"Thank you, we really appreciate it," Willow said.

"I'm happy to help," the tree said smiling. "Oh, and one more thing Auberon, remember that sometimes what you're looking for… is a whole lot closer than you think," she said, winking at him. "Good luck," the Lady Oak Tree whispered, as her face slowly disappeared beneath her tree bark.

After a couple of days traveling through the forest, they finally reached the grassy meadow the tree had spoken of. At the far end of the clearing, there was a short, brown bridge that was barely roped together through planks of wood.

"No way," Auberon said excitedly, under his breath, his eyes wide.

As Willow looked around, her eyes also lit up. "The Bridge of the Three Billy Goats Gruff! I can't believe we're actually here!" she said.

"Ever since I was little, I've always wanted to come see this place with my own two eyes!" Auberon said, trotting happily in a circle.

Willow smiled, too.

Willow came to an unsettling thought and she gasped. "Auberon, what if we meet the bridge troll?"

Auberon looked nervous. Even the billy goats from the Three Billy Goats Gruff barely made it past the troll, he thought to himself. "Let's just say we'll be better off if we don't meet him… that's for sure."

"My Dad's tales of this meadow were amazing, and I knew after about the dozenth time he had told it to me that I had to come see it for myself."

Willow nodded in agreement. "My parents also told me this story so many times it became my family's favorite story! Being here is like a walk through memory lane," she said, smiling at the idea of it.

They soon forgot about the troll, and were having so much fun. Auberon crossed the bridge about a dozen times, while Willow flitted between the ropes, enjoying every moment of it. Everything was great… that is, until they saw two strong hands pulling themselves up onto one end of the bridge. Sure enough, it was the bridge troll. He had an old, friendly face, although he did not look happy about being disturbed.

Willow flew as quickly as she could over to Auberon, and landed on his shoulder. She whispered nervously to Auberon, "I thought the troll floated down the river to his doom when the oldest billy goat knocked him off the bridge? At least, that's how my parents told the story."

But before Auberon could answer her, the troll gained his balance. "Who dares to cross my bridge?" wheezed the troll.

"Oh, uh… I'm Auberon, and this, this is Willow," Auberon stammered.

"I'm Finnian," said the old troll gruffly.

"Nice to make your acquaintance Finnian, but don't worry about us, we'll be leaving now!" Willow said flapping her wings, ready to fly away.

"Not so fast! What brings a bluebird and a horse over to my bridge?"

Finnian said with his hands on his knees, still trying to catch his breath.

"Well… actually, I'm a unicorn," said Auberon.

"A hornless unicorn? Hmm… that's new. I haven't seen that before," Finnian hesitated, "and trust me, I've seen a lot of things come through these woods!"

"I hear that a lot," Auberon admitted.

"We're here to go to the witch's house, so maybe she can give Auberon his horn," Willow told Finnian.

"Oh, well good luck with that. Maybe next time I see you, you'll have your horn," Finnian said to Auberon with compassion. "Now your bluebird friend Willow over there

doesn't have to worry about crossing my bridge because she can just fly right over. Trust me, I'm too old to chase her.

"I can't jump like I could back in the good old days. But you, Auberon? You don't have wings, so I don't have to let you pass. But, here's the thing," Finnian chuckled.

"What's so funny?" Auberon asked.

"It's just that… believe it or not, one time I was a lot like you," Finnian said.

Auberon tilted his head in confusion.

Finnian continued, "Others made fun of me, because, well… I was different," he said. "My parents were blue and yellow trolls, and they each placed a flag on this very bridge to represent them. It's just… I'm the only troll so far in all of my family's history that's a green troll. I used to be teased for it, but now I realize, the more colors in a rainbow, the prettier it becomes," Finnian said, sharing his heartfelt story with Auberon and Willow.

Auberon smiled at his tale. He understood what Finnian meant.

Finnian continued, "I don't want to be remembered as the troll that was too stubborn to let anybody cross my bridge. I'm old now. The least I can do is to help you Auberon, because I wish someone had given me a chance. A chance to prove that I was perfect just the way I am. Everyone deserves a chance, even hornless unicorns," Finnian said to Auberon with a grin and a wink. "So, I'm going to let you cross my bridge," he said with a genuine smile.

"You may pass," Finnian said, waving out his arm.

They traveled along the river, on their way to the witch's house. The raging river under Finnian's bridge soon tapered down to a peaceful stream, gently pulling autumn leaves silently through the forest.

Auberon and Willow stepped down the river bank, for a sip of water. They were astounded to see a graceful swan swimming by them, wearing a golden crown. There must have been at least twenty fuzzy ducklings following him in tow, like little yellow squires.

"Greetings from the Trickle Down, horse and bluebird," said the kingly swan. His line of downy admirers repeated, "Greetings!" exactly as the swan had said it.

Willow flew to his ear and whispered, "Well, my friend Auberon here is actually a unicorn. He just doesn't have his horn yet."

The swan took a second look at Auberon. "Ahhh, I see now," said the swan. His retinue of ducklings repeated, "I see now."

"Do you know that when I was born all the many ducks of Trickle Down Pond called me the one and only, 'Ugly Duckling?' I spent my early years devastated by it. But do you know what I see before me? I see a handsome unicorn with a fair friend! I would've given anything to have a friend like that."

Auberon said nothing. He felt a tinge of shame for wanting a horn so much. Now that he was out in the world, with a true friend, actually getting a horn was beginning to matter less than the adventure itself.

"Look at your reflection in the stream, and ask yourself, 'Would I rather be pretty, or wise and confident?'" the swan asked.

Then the swan began to swim down stream again. Not looking back, he said, "Good day, Auberon and kind bluebird... Look at me now, and remember what they once called me." And his ducky squires all repeated, "Look at me now! Look at me now!"

Auberon looked in the stream as the regal swan
said to do. He felt a little confused now.

"It's okay," Willow said. "We've come this far and the witch's house is right around the bend. You can think about it there."

Soon they could see the witch's house in the distance. As they drew closer, the delightful scent of warm baking bread wafted around them. It was a cozy wooden cottage, with a straw roof and brick chimney. Violets were planted in the front yard, and bougainvillea flower vines twisted their way up the walls and fence.

"Willow, wait!" Auberon said. "I'm not going to go in there."

"I don't understand, haven't you always wanted a horn?" Willow asked. "We've come all this way. Don't you at least want to go inside and talk with her?"

"Yes, I've always really wanted a horn, but I've learned something more important on the journey here."

"Really, well what is it?" Willow questioned.

Auberon smiled and said, "You know, throughout this entire journey, I was myself. We had so much fun along the way here. That swan inspired me. He taught me that you don't need to be beautiful to everyone else, because on the inside everyone is unique and special in their own way. When you think of a unicorn, you think of a horse with a horn. What's going to happen when we walk in there any-ways? I might get my horn. But besides that?

"The Oldest Oak Tree was right, even with a horn, I'll still be the same within. I'm the only one who can change any-thing about myself...

I have to learn to accept me for who I am,
with a horn — or without one."

Hearing this, Willow smiled. His powerful words had given her a new point of view. She closed her eyes to wipe a tear off her face with her wing, and as she opened them again, she was awestruck. She felt a cool breeze across her face, and in the breeze were golden sparkles. The fine, golden sparkles were carried through the air, and onto Auberon's head. Then, right before her eyes, the sparkles swirled collectively around his head faster and faster, until no more golden sparkles could be seen. Instead, there was a beautiful gleaming horn! It was by far the most spectacular horn that Willow had ever seen. She rubbed her eyes to make sure she wasn't dreaming.

Auberon noticed the astonishment on Willow's face. "What happened?" he asked.

"You… you… but how?" Willow looked around for the witch or anything that could explain what had just happened.

"Auberon, you have a horn!" Willow exclaimed.

"I what?" he asked, confused.

Just then, Auberon should have felt different, but he didn't. However, hearing Willow say this made him very happy. "I have a horn!" He galloped around the trees excitedly. "I have my horn!" he gleefully shouted again. Auberon was thrilled to have a horn, but it made him even happier knowing that finally he had truly accepted himself for who he was, with all of the love in his heart.

Willow gave him a compassionate hug, and flew around excitedly.

Then, Auberon paused for a moment. "But how did that happen?" he wondered aloud.

"I don't know," Willow said.

Auberon thought to himself. "Hmmm," he said. "I think I know who has the answer to my question."

Auberon bolted through the trees, and Willow zipped along beside him. "Who?" she asked, as she flew quickly to keep up.

"The Oldest Oak Tree."

"The one I took you to before?"

"No, it's a different one."

"Which one then?"

"The grandest, Oldest Oak Tree of them all," Auberon said.

"Have you met him before?" Willow asked.

"Yes."

"Okay, and why are we going to visit him again?" Willow wondered.

Auberon slowed down and said, "Because he'll know how I got my horn. After all, they are the Guardians of the Forest. If anybody will know how I got my horn, it'll be them."

As they were walking through the forest, they soon arrived again at the bridge where they had seen Finnian. Sitting in front of his house, below the bridge, was Finnian. At the sight of Auberon's horn, he smiled brightly and winked at Auberon in a congratulatory way as he was passing by.

They reached the Grove of Oak Trees in no time. Once again, the Oldest Oak Tree stretched out his face and popped his jaw into place.

"I see you got your horn," the Tree said, pretending to be surprised.

"Yes, I did!" Auberon said, proudly showing off its gleaming glow.

"So, since you have your horn, why exactly did you come to speak with me?" asked the Oldest Oak Tree.

Auberon raised his eyebrows. "Because I know you had something to do with it," he said confidently. How else would he magically get a horn? he thought, positive the Oak Tree had been involved.

"Well, maybe I did have something to do with it. But it wasn't just me, it was all of us," he said, gesturing with his branchy fingers to all of the other trees in the grove.

The Grand Oak tree began to explain, "Auberon, we had all been watching you grow up. So many unicorns take their beloved horns for granted, but we wanted you to appreciate yours, and maybe even show the other unicorns just how lucky they are to have horns. Horns are special, and we wanted the unicorns to realize that, and appreciate their beautiful gifts. So, we concealed your horn from you and everyone else to show you what it's like living without one."

The tree smiled at Auberon, and then continued his story.

"That's why when you were in the forest with Willow, as soon as you accepted yourself, and realized that you didn't need a horn to be you, your horn appeared. You didn't need us, or the witch to give you a horn. Your horn was with you all along."

"Remember when you came to me the first time, and I asked you a question that day?"

Auberon nodded his head. "You asked me if I really needed a horn to be happy, and I said that I did."

"This is why we wanted you to learn to accept yourself without having a horn, so you could see that you would still be happy even without one," the Grand Oak Tree wisely said.

"I have," Auberon said. "And I want to thank you for teaching me how to accept myself for who I am." Auberon rubbed his head against the tree bark as a sign of gratitude.

The tree laughed. "I'm proud of you, Auberon," he said as his face faded into his tree bark. Auberon has proven himself, by learning to accept who he is, thought the tree. I will always look after him, and now a part of him will always look at life in a whole new way.

As they were leaving the grove of magical trees, the Lady Oak Tree smiled warmly at Auberon and Willow. "I'm proud of you both, too," she said sweetly.

Auberon and Willow smiled at her thankfully.

"Thank you for sending us on the right path,
we found our way," Willow said.

"Anytime," the Lady Oak Tree responded. "Goodbye Willow.
Goodbye Auberon, although I'm sure it's not the last time we'll meet."

"Wow!" Auberon said to Willow. "They were looking after me that whole time. I guess it really is their job to protect this forest. They make it a better place for every creature. Now, I know why they did all of that. They truly are the 'Guardians of the Forest.'"

Willow smiled. "Yes they are."

Auberon and Willow decided to head home after speaking with the Oak Trees. It had been a journey that they would always remember. They formed a special bond and would be friends for life. As they walked, the trees thinned out, and more pines grew among the oaks. Birds soared through the sky happily, and cottontail rabbits bounced around. Playing in the grassy meadow was none other than the glamorous unicorns.

"Auberon?" someone shouted from the herd.

"Yes, it's me," Auberon said, as he galloped down into the grassy meadow, Willow flying by his side.

"Gosh, we haven't seen you around!" The unicorn that approached him was none other than Gideon.

Auberon opened his mouth to speak, but Gideon quickly interrupted him. "Listen," Gideon said. "I just want to say that we're sorry."

Auberon did not expect that. He looked around at all of the other unicorns, and they all looked back at him and nodded in agreement of Gideon's apology. "And most of all, I'm sorry. For everything. The way we treated you was mean, and it was wrong to pick on you. By the way, I like your horn!"

Auberon smiled. He could tell that all of the unicorns apologies were genuine.

"Friends?" Gideon asked, smiling.

"Friends," Auberon answered. The rest
of the herd came to join in as well.

Willow smiled at Auberon. She was happy that the other unicorns finally stopped teasing him, and from the look on his face, she could tell that he was happy, too. "I really did miss this place," she said warmly.

"Yeah, me too," Auberon said. "But I loved our time in the forest, and will always remember how much fun we had."

"Willow," Auberon said. "You know, I learned something important in the forest."

"Oh, what might that be?" Willow asked.

"It really wasn't about the destination, it was about the journey that I took with you that made the difference," Auberon said.

Willow felt a familiar breeze beneath her wings, and smiled genuinely at his heartfelt words.

The End

Acknowledgements

First of all, a big thank you to my family. Mom, Dad, and Levi, words can't even describe how grateful and thankful I am to have such an amazing, supportive family like you. I love y'all so much! Thank you for loving me, and supporting me every step of the way. Without you I don't know where I would be.

To my loveable canines: even though you can't read, I felt like I needed to include this acknowledgment. For sitting in my lap, or next to me while I wrote most of this book, for being some of the greatest cuddle buddies, and for loving me. I would like to thank my two wonderful dogs, Mordy, and his sister, Esther. I love both of you so much. In fact, both of you are next to me now as I'm writing this, so thanks for that, too!

Next, a huge thanks to Ryan Durney. You bring my story to life in so many ways with your amazing illustrations. I can't think of a better way to express my book's scenery than with your breathtaking art. Thank you for taking time to create these beautiful illustrations, and for spending countless hours helping me edit. You have taught me so much about writing along the way. Thank you also for brainstorming ideas with me. Lastly, thank you for taking a chance on me. Because I was a kid when I wrote this, and am writing this now. It was hard to find someone that would take me seriously and respect me as an author. Words can't describe how grateful I am for you helping me out on this wonderful book.

I would like to also thank Bradley Wilson for helping me edit my book in the beginning. I remember having amazing brainstorms with you while we would chat at BookPeople. Thanks for also helping me edit down my story. It was not an easy task. As an author - and you would know - it was only natural for me to want to keep every little bit of my story. Remember the apple tree? Yeah, that's what I thought. It was not easy to get rid of that one. Thank you for helping me make every part of my storyline count.

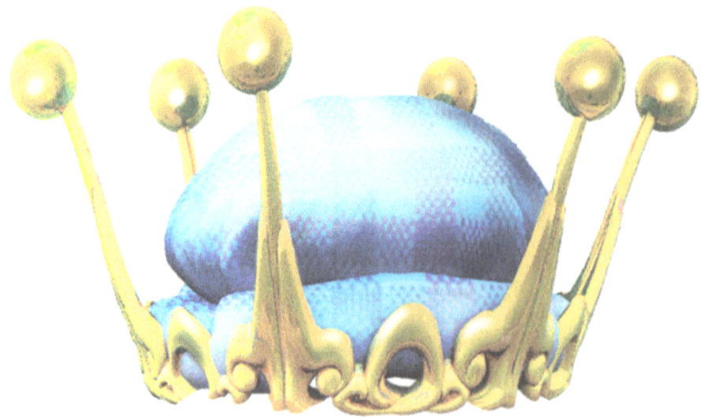

I would also like to thank Kirk Dando for giving great writing advice, and being the first person outside of my family to read my first draft and my final draft. You gave me some great tips along the way.

Thank you also to John Mackey for showing so much enthusiasm and listening to me read my story. The smile you had on your face while I was reading my book out loud made my day.

Thank you as well to my other family, friends, and more. Thanks to everyone who helped me throughout the process. Y'all supported me and were very encouraging on the journey of writing this amazing story. So thank you!

I would like to thank Anne Mazer and Ellen Potter, and their amazing book *Spilling Ink*. Without reading their book, I couldn't have possibly written my book. Once upon a time, I was struggling with my writing, I didn't know what to do, and I was completely inexperienced. So, my mom went to the bookstore and bought their book for me. She brought it home, and I thanked her, but at the time I didn't think I needed help at all. It sat on my bookshelf for a while, until one day my mom insisted that she read at least the first page to me. Reluctantly, I said okay. As she was reading it, I couldn't take my eyes away. It was amazing! Right then and there, it inspired me to write. My writer's block was over! I put my pen to my paper, and started spilling ink. *Spilling Ink* is one of the best books I have ever read. This book helped me tremendously, more than words can describe. So thank you.

Next, a big thank you to Chris Colfer, and his wonderful *Land of Stories* series. I read his first book in second grade and it inspired me to write. I had always loved to write, but for a long time I had fixed my plans on being a fashion designer. After reading his first book, it opened up my eyes. I realized how much I loved to write, especially fantasy. Your books are amazing — thank you for writing them!

Lastly, I would also like to thank the people that taught me how to write, and continue to teach me about writing and grammar. It's not an easy job. Thank you all my amazing teachers.

Rachel Hurt

My love for creative writing began to blossom when I was a child, and has only grown. It all started with my mom and I building fairy houses out of flowers and twigs and me being read endless stories, nightly, for countless years. Reading and writing became a pastime I was very fond of, and this love of mine eventually resulted in the beautiful book you are holding today.

When I was 11, I gave a TEDx talk about self-love and inner beauty, two values close to my heart that are also reflected in the morals of my book. I wrote *Guardians of the Forest* to inspire children and adults alike to love themselves for who they are through a fun story that follows the journey of Auberon.

I love playing tennis with friends and my mother, traveling with loved ones, creative writing, going to delicious restaurants, and exploring the city. I also cherish time spent with my friends, family, and my four dogs. I hope this book finds you well and allows a story sparked by my imagination–and crafted with love–to enable you to see self-love and acceptance in a new light and impact you for the better! Hope you enjoy! :)

With love, Rachel

P.S. One of my lovely dogs, Esther, sat in my lap while I typed the entirety of this book, as well, so she hopes you enjoy it, too!

Check out my website at: *Guardiansoftheforestbook.com*

Ryan Durney

I am an award-winning, full-time, free-lance illustrator focusing on children's books, fantasy, and science fiction as well as prehistoric subjects.

I use inks, paints and digital techniques to create a unique look. One review described my work as "pearlescent." My images are always straddling the fence between something classic and something that feels altogether new.

My accolades include: *Best of Fantasy, Society of Illustrators West #45,* as well as a *Mom's Choice Award* in 2011, 2012 and 2016. My work for *Princess Willow & the Magic Fairy Brush* won "Creative Child Magazine's Product of the Year: 2016." I was the featured illustrator of over 36 issues of *ODYSSEY Sci-Fi Magazine,* and was the sole illustrator chosen for their retrospective collection. All-in-all, though, I count being voted in by the kids for a *Children's Choice Award* as my favorite recognition.

In my spare time, when I'm not walking our dog, Pooka, I write and illustrate projects like *Birds of Lore,* and *Mirrors of the Abyss*.

ryandurney.com / @Unknown_Tome / Hire An Illustrator: http://illo.cc/44158 / Facebook: www.facebook.com/pages/Unknown-Tome-Ryan-Durney-Illustration